VERSUS THE VOLCANO!

ZONDERKIDZ

Larryboy Versus the Volcano!
Copyright © 2004 Big Idea, Inc. VEGGIETALES®, character names, likenesses and other indicia are trademarks of Big Idea, Inc. All rights reserved.

Requests for information should be addressed to:
Zonderkidz, *Grand Rapids, Michigan 49530*

Library of Congress Cataloging-in-Publication Data

Peterson, Doug.
   Larry versus the volcano / by Doug Peterson. — 1st ed.
     p. cm.
   Summary: Larryboy takes a vacation on a volcanic island for superheroes and learns a lesson about including others when he is excluded by his favorite superhero buddies like Lemon Twist and Electro-Melon.
   ISBN 978-0-310-70728-8
   [1. Heroes — Fiction. 2. Vacations — Fiction. 3. Christian life — Fiction.] I. Title.
   PZ7.P44334Lap 2004
   [Fic] — dc22

                              2004000251

All Scripture quotations, unless otherwise indicated, are taken from the Holy Bible, *New International Version®, NIV®*. Copyright © 1973, 1978, 1984 by Biblica, Inc.™ Used by permission of Zondervan. All rights reserved worldwide.

Any Internet addresses (websites, blogs, etc.) and telephone numbers printed in this book are offered as a resource. They are not intended in any way to be or imply an endorsement by Zondervan, nor does Zondervan vouch for the content of these sites and numbers for the life of this book.

Written: Doug Peterson
Editor: Cindy Kenney
Cover and interior illustrations: Michael Moore
Cover design and art direction: Paul Conrad, Karen Poth
Interior design: Holli Leegwater, John Trent, and Karen Poth

Printed in the United States of America

VeggieTales

LARRYBOY™

VERSUS THE VOLCANO!

WRITTEN BY
DOUG PETERSON

ILLUSTRATED BY
MICHAEL MOORE

BASED ON THE HIT VIDEO SERIES: LARRYBOY
CREATED BY PHIL VISCHER
SERIES ADAPTED BY TOM BANCROFT

ZONDERkidz

ZONDERVAN.com/
AUTHOR**TRACKER**
follow your favorite authors

TABLE OF CONTENTS

CHAPTER 1

A ROCKY BEGINNING

Larry the Cucumber
couldn't believe it was happening.
He was actually having a picnic with Vicki
Cucumber, the only girl to ever make his heart
skip a beat. For a mild-mannered janitor like
Larry, the day was postcard picture-perfect.

Larry and Vicki were on the grassy side of
Bumbly Mountain, which offered a great view of
Bumblyburg. There was only one glitch. Larry couldn't
come up with a thing to talk about.

"Um...did you know that a cockroach can live for
several weeks without its head?" asked Larry. He was
reading from his list of "Conversation Topics," prepared
especially for times like this.

"Uh...no, I didn't," Vicki answered.

Larry smiled and looked around nervously.

Then he snuck another peek at his Conversation Topics. "Did you know that houseflies like to—?"

"Maybe we should eat," Vicki suggested, quickly changing the subject.

"Good idea," agreed Larry, opening the picnic basket. He pulled out a chicken drumstick. "I made the chicken myself. It's an old family recipe that—"

"AHHHHHHHHHHHHHHHHHH!" Vicki suddenly screamed out of the blue.

Larry looked down at his chicken. "It doesn't taste that bad. You should just try it—"

"It's not the food!" Vicki yelled. "It's *that!*"

Larry looked up the hill. A giant boulder had cracked loose from the side of the mountain and was heading right toward them.

With swift, cucumber reflexes, Larry shoved Vicki out of the way. But he didn't have time to save himself. The rock was upon him!

"Larry!" shouted Vicki, closing her eyes. She couldn't look as Larry the Cucumber was about to become squash.

Larry flipped forward on top of the rock as it raced downhill. But his troubles were just beginning. Trying to stay on top of a rolling stone was like running on a very dangerous treadmill. Larry rode the boulder as it barreled down the mountain at breakneck speed—emphasis on breaking necks.

The boulder was headed straight for Bumbly Park, which was packed with Veggies attending the annual Taste of Bumblyburg Celebration. The crowd was an easy target for an out-of-control boulder.

When the rock came upon a small ledge, it went flying, flipping Larry high into the air. The rock crashed back down onto the ground with a **THUD** that shook the mountain like a dinosaur's step.

Larry also hit the ground with an **"OOF!"** and began to roll downhill, out of control. He somersaulted down the side of the mountain, over and over and over.

Kind of like a boulder, come to think of it.

The chase was on.

CHAPTER 2

BETWEEN A ROCK AND A HARD PLACE

Screaming Veggies scattered like ants as the big boulder smashed its way through Bumbly Park. The boulder pulverized a taco stand, flattened a hot dog cart, and headed straight for a group of innocent and unsuspecting Cub Sprouts!

Fortunately, Larry had recently taken a special training course on how to switch into his superhero costume while swimming, skydiving, playing hop-scotch, and...amazingly...while rolling down a hill totally out of control. By the time Larry the Janitor had rolled through the crowd in Bumbly Park, he had changed into Bumblyburg's most famous, most purplish hero of all time...LARRYBOY!

"I AM THAT HERO!" he shouted, firing one of his supersuction ears.

THONK!

The plunger hit the boulder and held fast. Larryboy was sure that the tether cord stretching from the plunger back to his head would be enough to stop the boulder. But he underestimated the power of the rock. The boulder yanked Larryboy up into the air.

The rock closed in on the Cub Sprouts, who were now frozen with fear.

Meanwhile, Larryboy's tether cord wrapped 'round and 'round the rolling boulder as Larryboy flew behind in midair, being pulled in closer and closer to the boulder— like string around a ball.

ZIP!

Larryboy sent a second supersuction ear zipping toward the side of a nearby bagel truck. **THONK!** The purple protector anchored himself to the side of the truck, hoping to slow the rampaging boulder on the other side.

Only one problem...

Larryboy felt like he was being torn apart between the rock and the bagel truck! As the truck tipped back on its rear wheels, the doors swung open and thousands of bagels came rolling out.

But the cords held fast, finally bringing the boulder to a stop...just inches before crushing the Cub Sprouts.

As the crowd dodged different flavored bagels, they let out a cheer, and Larryboy smiled in relief.

"Thank you, thank you, it was nothing," our hero said, pulling out a chicken drumstick, which had become caught in his cape while he changed into his costume.

"AHHHHHHHHHHHHHHH!" the people screamed.

"What is it about my chicken that causes such a reaction?" Larryboy asked, staring at his drumstick.

"It's not the chicken, Larryboy!" shouted Officer Olaf.

"It's that!"

Larryboy spun around and looked right into the angry eyes of the boulder! *"Eyes?"* said Larryboy. "Since when do boulders have eyes?"

"I not only have eyes," spoke the rock. "I also have a mouth."

With that, the boulder laughed and breathed out the worst stream of bad breath that Larryboy had ever whiffed. The rock's breath was burning hot and spicy, with just a hint of dog breath, dirty gym socks, and unwashed weasel smell.

In fact, the odor was so powerful that Larryboy fell over backwards, completely unconscious.

With Larryboy out of the picture, the rock let loose another evil laugh that would have scored high in the annual Villainous Laugh Contest at the Bumblyburg State Fair. Then the rock rolled right through the side of the Scuba-Tuba Superstore—the largest store in the world devoted to underwater diving equipment and tubas.

"Let's rock and roll!" laughed the rock, stealing scuba gear right and left.

But Larryboy wasn't defeated yet. The wobbly super-hero regained consciousness and spotted the boulder driving a forklift that loaded scuba gear onto a truck.

"Yo, Rocky! Release that scuba gear!" Larryboy shouted, trying to strike a dramatic pose (which was hard to do while dazed and dizzy).

The boulder wheeled around in surprise. "So the pickle boy woke up! You know what you get when you wake up, don't you? DRAGON BREATH!" The boulder smiled wickedly and breathed another mouthful of deadly odors.

The last thing Larryboy remembered smelling was a mixture of superheated air, tangy spices, and spoiled milk. Then everything went dark.

CHAPTER 3

GETTING AWAY FROM IT ALL

"It's a good thing
you have a spare costume. This one
may be ruined," said Archibald, Larryboy's
faithful servant.

Archie was trying to scrub the foul smell
from Larryboy's costume, while our cucumber hero
lounged around in his bathrobe, sipping Slushees.
It was nighttime, and Larryboy was back inside the
Larrycave.

"By the way, what did that rocky rascal get away
with?" Larryboy asked sleepily.

"He stole every piece of scuba and snorkeling gear
in the store, Master Larry."

"Scuba gear?" Larryboy asked, puzzled. "What
would a rock do with scuba gear?"

"I'm not certain. First, tell me about your time

with Vicki. Were you enjoying yourselves before the boulder hit the scene?"

Larryboy's eyes lit up. "Vicki and I had a great time, Archie. I just wish I didn't always have to save Bumblyburg so often—and at the worst of times! It's exhausting." Larryboy took another sip of his chocolate mocha-mint vanilla swirl frozen drink.

"I see," said Archie, madly scrubbing the Larryboy costume.

"I've been thinking that I could use a vacation," Larryboy said, sinking deeper into his cushy couch. "I need time off when I can't be interrupted."

"A vacation would be nice," Archie agreed, scrubbing even harder.

Larryboy sprang from the couch. "I'm glad you agree! I know just the place to go." He unfolded a large, colorful brochure. "It's called Superhero Island!"

Archie set aside the soggy costume, took the brochure, and sat down to read it. "Where did you get this, Master Larry?"

"Someone stuck it on the windshield of the Larrymobile. Doesn't Superhero Island sound great? Beautiful beaches! Scuba diving! Gourmet dining!"

Archie continued to read:

TIRED OF LEAPING TALL BUILDINGS
OR RUNNING FASTER THAN A SPEEDING LOCOMOTIVE?
DO ORDINARY PEOPLE EXPECT YOU TO SAVE THE WORLD,
EVEN IN THE MIDDLE OF YOUR FAVORITE CARTOON?
YOU **DESERVE** A BREAK TODAY ON
SUPERHERO ISLAND!

YOU'LL BE SURROUNDED BY THE **GREATEST,**
MOST HEROIC, AND **IMPORTANT**
PEOPLE ON THE PLANET—OTHER SUPERHEROES!
SUPERHERO ISLAND IS AN EXCLUSIVE RESORT,
SPECIALLY CREATED FOR **SUPER PEOPLE ONLY.**

IMAGINE:
AN ENTIRE WEEK WITH
THE BEST OF THE BEST!
YOU'LL HAVE A PERFECT TIME WHEN
YOU'RE WITH **PERFECT** PEOPLE!

"It sounds a little snooty to me," said Archie.

"Oh, don't be a stick-in-the-mud," laughed Larryboy.

Archie shook his head. "Well…if this is where you really want to go for vacation, I'll pack the bags."

"Superhero Island, here we come!"

CHAPTER 4

TURNING UP THE HEAT

A thousand miles away from the Larrycave was a cave of a completely different sort. This was a dark, secluded cave, tucked away on a deserted jungle island. Torches and multicolored lava lamps eerily lit up the cave.

This was none other than the secret hideout of the world-famous Chili Pepper. However, Chili Pepper was not world-famous for being a supervillain, as you're probably thinking. No one even knew about Chili's wicked ways. Instead, Chili Pepper was famous for being "the Snooty Gourmet," a television chef who gave tips on how to make chili a hundred different ways.

Chili's sidekick was Coconut, a muscular thug who dreamed of someday becoming much more than just a sidekick. He wanted to be a supervillain himself. In fact, he was taking an evil genius correspondence course and was busily doing his homework.

"Um, Chili Pepper, what do you think about this question?" Coconut said, holding up his quiz. "Question 4 says: 'If you had evil mutant power, what would you use it for? (A) To take over the world; (B) To wreak havoc and destruction; or (C) To floss regularly?' I was thinking the answer might be D."

"D? There is no D," said Chili Pepper.

"I know. But I think this is a trick question. D is an invisible answer. They put it in just to fool me."

"Ah...good thinking," said Chili Pepper, rolling his eyes. "Then maybe you should fill out all of your answers in invisible ink."

"Great idea!" grinned Coconut.

Chili Pepper stood at his deluxe stove, testing his latest chili recipe. He was famous for making the hottest, spiciest chili in the universe—chili so spicy that it brought tears to your eyes from a block away.

"By the way, Coconut, how many superheroes have signed up to come to our island retreat?" Chili Pepper asked, tasting his hot concoction.

Coconut set aside his quiz to check the registration

book. "One hundred and thirty-five superheroes are coming to Superhero Island, boss. That's a lot of spandex!"

"That's almost every superhero in the world," snickered Chili Pepper. "Little do they know that Superhero Island is really a Tourist Trap! Emphasis on the word 'trap'!"

"Good one, Boss!" Coconut laughed. Then his smile vanished as a thought crossed his mind—a rare event. "But what about this mysterious volcanic rock I've heard about? Do you think this creature will be mad when it finds out what we're doing to the island's volcano? Personally, that rock scares me."

"Don't worry about a piece of stone," said Chili Pepper, stirring the chili. "Let's concentrate on the superheroes. They don't realize that I've cooked up one big surprise for them. When they arrive, they're going to get a taste of my awesome power!"

Chili Pepper's laugh echoed through the caves, rumbling ominously throughout the entire island.

CHAPTER 5

AN INVITATION TO DANGER

Larry the Janitor had never seen Bob the Tomato this way before. Bob had always been the super-serious, hardworking editor of the *Daily Bumble* newspaper.

But not today.

Today, Bob the Tomato was wearing a Hawaiian shirt, a big straw hat, and sunglasses. Polynesian music floated out of Bob's office as Larry the Janitor prepared to mop his floor.

"What's up?" Larry asked.

"I'll tell you what's up!" Bob exclaimed, taking Larry's mop and dancing around the room with it.

"I'm going on the assignment of a lifetime! I'm off to Superhero Island!"

Larry almost blurted out, "So am I!" But he

caught himself just in time. You see, no one but Archie knew that Larry was much more than a mild-mannered janitor for the *Daily Bumble*. No one else knew that he was also LARRYBOY!

"That's nice," he said instead.

"Vicki and I have been invited to Superhero Island to do an exclusive report on this new resort for superheroes," Bob explained, popping open his luggage and checking to make sure he had everything. "I'm doing the story, and Vicki is taking photos. Even though it's work, it'll feel like a vacation."

"Well, don't forget your sunblock," Larry said, pulling a tube out of Bob's suitcase and handing it to him. "You're already looking pretty red."

"I'm a tomato, Larry. Tomatoes *are* red!"

"Oh. Right."

"This is going to be the most fun assignment ever!" Bob shouted as he spread the sunscreen on his face. "Hey! This is minty-smelling sunscreen. I like it!"

Larry took a closer look at the tube that he had just handed to Bob. Then he quickly ducked out of the room as he spotted Vicki about to enter Bob's office.

"How come you smeared toothpaste all over your face,

Chief?" Vicki asked as she entered the room.

As Larry hopped onto the elevator, he heard Bob shout, "LARRY!"

So much for Bob's good mood. He quickly pushed the "down" button.

CHAPTER 6
VACATION FEVER

You probably know what it's like on the last day of school before vacation. Well, that's pretty much what it was like in Larryboy's Superhero 101 class later that day at Bumblyburg Community College.

Most of the superheroes didn't have their minds on their studies or their eyes on their instructor, Bok Choy. Their eyes were on the clock, and their minds were on Superhero Island. Almost every superhero in the class was planning to go on vacation to the island.

The Scarlet Tomato sat in class wearing snorkeling gear. Electro-Melon had stuffed a surfboard into his school backpack. And Larryboy was blowing up a huge, inflatable rubber ducky.

ceived the same Superhero Island

ne of them was convinced they were

ST and wanted the perfect getaway

pie.

superhero's pride inflated just as rapidly as the
rubber ducky that Larryboy was blowing up.

"Larryboy, I hate to take the air out of your duck,
but would you read today's lesson from the Superhero
Handbook?" said Bok Choy.

"Mmmm?" Larryboy asked, his mouth still puffing on
the slowly inflating raft.

"Please read Section 45, paragraph 12, line 16 in your Superhero Handbook."

"MMMMMMM MMMMM MM MMMMMM MMM MMMM," Larryboy mumbled, reading from the Handbook.

"Perhaps you could stop inflating your raft while you read," Bok Choy suggested.

Larryboy let out a big sigh, reluctantly releasing his mouth from the duck's blower-upper thingie. Instantly, all of the air gushed out, and the duck took off like a balloon rocket.

"DUCK!"

The deflating duck flew wildly around the room, bouncing off walls, knocking over the globe, swooping around Electro-Melon's surfboard, crashing into a stack of books, and finally winding up on top of Bok Choy's desk.

"Oops," said Larryboy.

"Please proceed," urged Bok Choy patiently.

Larryboy stood up and read: "Don't be proud. Be willing to be a friend of people who aren't considered important. Don't think that you are better than others."

"Very good, Larryboy," said their wise instructor. "As the Handbook says, when we think we're better than others, we become proud and arrogant. And when we're arrogant, we don't want to be seen with people we think are unimportant. We exclude them and don't treat them as God wants us to."

Bok Choy paused because no one was paying attention. Every superhero was watching the clock, counting the seconds to when the bell would ring. So Bok Choy yanked the clock off the wall and hung it around his neck like a giant medallion. That way, at least the students would be looking in his direction.

He continued, "When we exclude others, we become filled with even more pride and arrogance. So remember that EVERYONE is important in God's eyes. As superheroes, you should set an example of this."

Bok Choy stopped and sighed. "Did any of you hear one word I said?"

Nope. Every eye was waiting for the second hand on the clock to make one final sweep. 5-4-3-2-1...

RINNNNNNNNGGGGG!

The bell had rung. Class was over.

"Vacation time!"

Like a stampede of crazed water buffaloes, the entire class stormed out of the room. If Bok Choy hadn't done his famous ninja triple flip into the air, he might have been trampled to the ground. Instead, he wound up safely on top of his desk, nestled securely inside Larryboy's rubber duck.

"I know exactly how you feel," he said to the duck. "After a class like today, I'm pretty deflated, too."

CHAPTER 7

SECOND-CLASS CITIZENS

Chili Pepper and his sidekick, Coconut, stood on the edge of the Superhero Island runway, watching superhero after superhero arrive by supersonic jet, atomic-powered helicopter, or rocket backpack. Larryboy swooped in on his Larryplane.

"De plane! De plane!" Coconut shouted as each plane hit the runway. "De plane! De plane! De—"

"Coconut, knock it off," Chili Pepper said.

"Sorry, Boss. But I always wanted to say that."

As Larryboy and Archie hopped out of the cockpit, several island girls rushed up to take their luggage, hand them a glass of lemonade, and welcome them to Superhero Island. Each girl wore a sticker that said, "HELLO, My name is _____. I'm not as important as *you*."

"Didn't I tell you this would be great?" said Larryboy. "I feel relaxed already!"

"I'm glad *someone's* relaxed," said Archibald. He wasn't feeling very comfortable disguised as Larryboy's airplane mechanic, wearing bib overalls, a bandana, and grease streaked across his face—probably the only mechanic to wear a monocle.

The island was paradise—the thick rain forest was overrun with monkeys and colorful birds. The water was clear, the waterfalls plentiful, and beautiful streams cut across the landscape from a huge, majestic mountain in the center of the island.

"That's Mount Superhero," announced Chili Pepper, as he and Coconut welcomed their guests.

"And that's Chili Pepper, the Snooty Gourmet," whispered Larryboy to Archie. "I watch his cooking show on TV all the time. If he's running things, the food's gonna be great! Chili-filled donuts...chili pancakes...chili chocolate cake...!"

"He must like his chili hot and spicy," noted Archie, as Chili Pepper tossed a breath mint into his mouth. "His breath could peel wallpaper."

Everything on the island was picture-perfect postcard.

Except for one slight hitch.

As the superheroes lined up to enter the resort, Chili Pepper asked each one of them a question.

"What makes you a superhero?" Chili asked Larryboy's friend Lemon Twist.

"At an early age, I discovered that I had the ability to control the air within a one-foot radius around my body," Lemon Twist said. "I can create gale-force winds."

"Nice, very nice," said Chili Pepper. "You may enter."

Lemon Twist hopped forward, and a robotic arm shot out from the wall, planting an invisible stamp smack in the center of her forehead.

As each superhero entered the resort, it was always the same question. "What makes you a superhero?"

Unfortunately, some didn't make the cut.

"My super power is shooting straw wrappers for distances up to a half mile using a highly refined laser guidance system," said a lima bean who called himself Straw Man.

Chili Pepper scoffed. "You call that a superhero power? Sorry, you're not important enough. Go home."

In desperation, Straw Man pulled out one of his laser-guided straws. But before he could fire off a single wrapper, a robotic foot came out of the wall and booted Straw Man out of line.

"Some people have all the nerve," Larryboy whispered to Archie. "They think they're an important superhero when they're NOT. Party crashers."

"And what makes you a superhero?" Chili Pepper asked when Larryboy finally reached the front of the line.

"My supersuction ears!" Larryboy declared proudly, his cape flapping in the breeze. "I even have my own line of action figures. I AM THAT HERO!"

"But what is your super power?" Chili Pepper asked.

Larryboy was stunned. "Super power? Well..."

"Some superheroes don't have special powers," Archie chimed in. "Instead, Larryboy uses amazing gadgets and vehicles, such as the Larryplane and the Larrymobile. I should know. I work on them. See the grease?"

"I've protected Bumblyburg from dastardly villains for years," Larryboy added, panic rising. "You can't exclude me from the island!"

"Calm down," said Chili Pepper. "You can stay on the island, but I'm afraid you won't be included in the First Class section of our exclusive resort. Because you don't have special powers, you and your mechanic will have to stay in the Second Class section."

Larryboy let out a big sigh of relief. "Second Class section. I can live with that. That's not so bad. That's—"

Suddenly, the robotic boot gave both Larryboy and Archie a big wallop. Kicked high in the air, the caped cucumber and his mechanic landed head-first in the sand—right in front of the Second Class entrance.

Larryboy popped his head out of the sand and looked at the gate to the Second Class section. The gate was falling off of its rusty hinges.

"Carry yer own luggage," snapped a snooty servant, walking by with his nose in the air.

"Are we having fun yet?" Archie asked, spitting sand from his mouth.

CHAPTER 8

RECIPE FOR DISASTER

Later that night, Coconut was going nuts. Freaking out. He dashed into their secret cave hideout, only to find Chili Pepper calmly cooking another gigantic pot of chili.

"What is it now, big guy?" Chili asked, rolling his eyes.

"That rock! He's here. On the island. I saw a rock, and it stared at me with EYES! It was really creepy!"

"So what's the big deal?" asked Chili Pepper.

"That volcanic rock is going to be furious when he finds out what we're doing to the island's volcano!"

"You worry too much, Coconut. It's not good for your digestion. Now read that recipe back to me."

Although Chili Pepper liked hot food, he was one cool customer.

"Which recipe?" Coconut said, flipping through the Evil Genius Cookbook.

"You know, the recipe for my greatest culinary creation of all time: Volcano Chili!"

"Oh. Right. Here it is," said Coconut. "First step: Fill the inside of a volcano with 23 zillion gallons of chili. Stir vigorously."

"Done," said Chili Pepper.

"Second step: Add 14 trillion pounds of shredded cheese."

"Done."

"Third," continued Coconut, "while the chili simmers, bake 33 billion giant dinner rolls, then add them to the volcanic mixture."

"That's also been done."

"Turn on the invisible force field to trap everyone on the island."

"Check," said Chili Pepper.

"Make sure your escape pod is ready," read Coconut.

"Done."

"Finally, bring chili to a boil, then trigger several under-ground explosions. A volcanic eruption should occur within an hour. Serves 135."

"Aha! Setting the timer for an explosion is the only thing left for us to do," said Chili Pepper, pushing a button on a remote-control device.

WHIRRRRRRR...KA-CHUNK!

That was the sound of an entire cave wall sliding open to reveal what looked like the largest pop can ever created. The can was as big as a house, and it contained Chili Pepper's personal brand of pop—Chili-Cola, a spicy, chili-flavored soft drink.

"That's one big can," said Coconut. "What's it got to do with explosions?"

"Watch and learn," said Chili. He pushed another button, and a huge mechanical hand shot out of the wall. It grabbed the monstrous can and began to shake...and shake...and shake.

"**OOOOOOOOOO**, I get it," said Coconut. "Shake this can, and it explodes when you open it."

"That's right," laughed Chili Pepper villainously. "We're going to let this can shake all day. When the top is popped tomorrow, this carbonated time bomb is going to fizz and explode, setting off a chain reaction. The exploding pop can will trigger earthquakes, causing the volcano to blow, which will destroy the entire island! Every superhero here will be trapped as the island slowly sinks into the sea."

Coconut and Chili Pepper clambered up a spiral staircase that ran alongside the monstrous pop can.

"What should I set it for, Boss?" Coconut asked, peering at the timer on the shaking machine.

"Fourteen hours should give us plenty of time. We've got to make our guests feel at home...before they're blown to bits."

The countdown began. The island had become a giant, ticking time bomb, ready to pop its top.

By the following morning, disaster would be served.

CHAPTER 9

BEACH BUMMER

The next day, Bob and Vicki found Larryboy and Archie on the Second Class beach, trying to catch a little sun.

While Vicki snapped photos, Bob pulled out his notebook and peppered Larryboy with questions. "So how's everything on the Second Class side?"

"Is this on the record?" Larryboy asked.

Bob nodded.

"Well, I'm glad you asked, Bob! Things are LOUSY on the Second Class side of the island. Service is horrible! The dinners come out of vending machines. And there are no maids to clean up the rooms."

"He's correct," added Archie. "So many things on this side of the island are broken that a roll of duct tape is left in every room, right next to the Standard Superhero Handbook (which is also taped together)."

Even the Second Class beach was a mess. The sand was covered with little burrs that stuck to your body. And every beach chair was patched together with...what else? Duct tape.

But that wasn't the worst of it.

"HOWDY! HOWDY! HOWDY! My name is Tourist-Man!"

That was the worst of it.

Tourist-Man was a carrot whose super power was his ability to put people to sleep with his boring vacation pictures. He wore a bright Hawaiian shirt, lugged around three huge pieces of luggage filled with photo albums and vacation slides, and spoke so loudly that you wished he had a mute button.

"SAY CHEESE!" yelled Tourist-Man obnoxiously.

FLASH!

Did I mention that he also carried around a camera and took flash pictures in your face approximately every five seconds?

"I guess I'll be on the Second Class side of the beach from now on!" Tourist-Man shouted, setting up his slide projector right there on the beach. "I just got voted off of the other side of the island. CAN YOU BELIEVE IT?"

"I can't imagine why," said Bob sarcastically.

"Say, I like your camera!" Tourist-Man noted, when he spotted Vicki's camera equipment. "Does it have a flash as bright as mine? SAY CHEESE!"

FLASH!

Vicki staggered backwards as the light left her seeing spots. "You can get sunburn from a flash that bright," she said, running into a nearby palm tree.

"Isn't it great?" beamed Tourist-Man.

Quietly escaping Tourist-Man's chaotic presence, Larryboy wandered over to the huge privacy wall that separated the First Class side from the Second Class side of the beach. The voices of happy, laughing superheroes on the other side infuriated him. He felt terribly left out.

"THAT'S IT!" Larryboy scowled. "I'm not taking this any more! I'm going over the wall!"

With that, the caped cucumber climbed up the wall and squeezed beneath the barbed wire top. Then he leaped onto the First Class side of the beach...

...and found himself in a whole new world.

CHAPTER 10

THE SUPER SNUB

On the First Class side, the beach was as white as snow. Not a burr in sight. Servants swarmed everywhere, serving every superhero's desire. The First Class superheroes also had their pick of jet skis, motorboats, sailboats, scuba gear, and even jet packs.

Larryboy tried to blend in with the First Class crowd but was immediately spotted.

"What ya'll doing here, Larryboy?" asked Sweet Potato, a down-home Southern superhero who happened to be as strong as a Mack Truck.

"Sssshhhhh, I'm just hanging out," whispered Larryboy.

"Hey, Larryboy, what's up?" asked Lemon Twist. "Aren't you

supposed to be on the Second Class side? Or have you developed special powers in the past day?"

The Scarlet Tomato, following just behind Lemon Twist, chuckled. "I don't-a think Chili Pepper will be happy if he sees-a you here. This side is-a for the more important superheroes, you know."

"You don't believe that, do you?" Larryboy said.

"Well, it does make some sense," said Sweet Potato. "I mean, if ya'll didn't have your contraptions, you wouldn't be much of a superhero, would you, sweet thing? We're superheroes, with or without contraptions. That makes us more important."

"As my uncle Guido would-a say, 'If you-a got it, you-a got it.' And we-a got it," said the Scarlet Tomato.

"What seems to be the trouble here?" boomed a loud voice from directly behind Larryboy. It was Coconut, the bouncer.

Coconut took one look at Larryboy and nearly split his shell. "WHAT are you doing on the First Class side of the beach, pickle boy?"

"It's really very simple…"

"Save your breath, gadget guy!" said Coconut as he hurled Larryboy up and over the wall.

Back on the Second Class side of the beach, Bob, Vicki, Archie, and Tourist-Man watched as Larryboy came sailing over the wall, landing headfirst in the sand.

"SAY CHEESE!" Tourist-Man exclaimed, clicking photos of Larryboy upside down in the sand.

FLASH!

Larryboy felt rejected and all-around lousy...until he realized there was something under the sand where he landed.

"This is strange," he said—although with his head in the sand it sounded more like, **"MMMM MM MMMMMMM."**

Archie helped Larryboy out of the sand. Larryboy repeated himself. "Guys! There's something here!"

As the group gathered around, Larryboy used the toy beach shovel on his utility belt to dig wildly in the sand. About a foot below the surface, he uncovered a metal trapdoor.

"I bet I know what *that* is," Larryboy said. "It's a secret passageway to the First Class side of the beach."

Bob whistled softly. "You could be right."

"I'll check it out."

The caped cucumber yanked open the hatch and leaped in—which was not a good move. He should have looked before he leaped.

"*Yikes!*"

Yikes was right. Larryboy found himself tumbling toward a stream of very hot liquid. And if he wasn't mistaken, it looked an awful lot like lava. Red-hot lava. Volcanic lava.

"ARCHIE! HEEEEEEEEEELP!"

CHAPTER 11

THE TIME BOMB

Larryboy fired off
both of his supersuction ears. The
first suction cup hit a slippery stalactite in
the underground cave but didn't catch hold.
(Stalactites are those pointy rocks that hang
down from cave ceilings like fangs.) The second
plunger caught the cave's ceiling just in time,
preventing Larryboy from taking a very hot lava bath.
The caped cucumber dangled upside down from
the tether cord, only inches above the thick, steam-
ing liquid. "SAY CHEESE!" called Tourist-Man from the
trapdoor above.

FLASH!

"Excuse me, Tourist-Man," said Archie, bumping
the carrot aside as he peeked down into the cave.
"Are you all right, Larryboy? What's down there?"

"Well…at first I thought it was lava," said Larryboy. "But after I took a couple of sniffs, I think it smells an awful lot like chili."

Larryboy stuck out his tongue and took a taste. "Mmmmmmmm, tastes like chili!" He took another slurp.

"Easy, Larryboy, you've already had four bowls of Chili Crunch cereal this morning," said Archie. "You don't want to spend the rest of this adventure in the bathroom."

"Good point. Do you suppose Chili Pepper is behind all of this chili?" Larryboy asked.

"Most likely," said Archie. "But I'm not sure why."

"There's a ladder leading down here. Why don't you climb down and help me find some clues!" Larryboy called. "There's also a path alongside this stream."

Archie, Bob, and Vicki clambered down the ladder and released Larryboy from the ceiling. Tourist-Man wasn't far behind, groaning as he dragged along his three giant pieces of luggage and his camera.

"Do you have to carry luggage everywhere you go?" Vicki asked.

"Wouldn't be caught dead without it," said Tourist-Man, wheeling around and nearly knocking Bob into the chili-lava with one of his suitcases. Larryboy caught Bob

just in time by using a supersuction ear.

"Let's follow the cave's trail," said Vicki.

So the adventurers took off, bouncing along the underground pathway. The stream of chili-lava bubbled and steamed, making the tunnel as hot as a sauna. Along the trail, the heroes didn't even need a flashlight because Tourist-Man's nonstop flashing went off every few seconds, providing plenty of illumination.

"What in the world...?" gasped Bob. The little group came across a second stream. Only this was a stream of melted cheese. The cheese merged with the chili, creating one great big gurgling river of molten food.

"SAY CHEESE!" Tourist-Man bellowed. "Get it? Say cheese?"

Larryboy found another ladder, which led to an upper level lit by torches. The group marched through two large rooms until they came across the most shocking sight of all. A large mechanical hand was wildly shaking a monstrous pop can.

"Chili-Cola," smiled Larryboy. "My favorite."

"But why the mega pop can?" asked Bob. "What's it for?"

Archie climbed the spiral staircase alongside the giant pop can, studying the shaking contraption every step of the way. "I hate to say this," said Archie. "But this is a Fizz Bomb. The pop can is set to open in approximately one hour."

"You mean...?" gasped Bob.

"Yes. When the mechanical hand opens, this pop can is going to explode!"

"But why?" asked Vicki.

"It's probably set to trigger an earthquake or volcanic eruption," said Archie.

"Earthquakes! Volcanoes! Finally, I'm going to have a vacation slide show that won't put people to sleep," grinned Tourist-Man.

Larryboy hopped up beside Archie. "Is there any way we can disconnect the pop can before it explodes?"

"Sure there is," said Archie. "By cutting the wire on the machine...the correct wire."

Archie nodded toward a tangle of wires, which led from the timer to the shaking device.

"The big question is," paused Archie, "do we cut the red wire? Or do we cut the blue one?"

"What happens if we cut the wrong one?" asked Vicki.

"KA-BOOM!" shouted Tourist-Man happily.

"That would be an accurate conclusion," Archie stated.

CHAPTER 12

SAY CHEESE!

Larryboy removed a pair of wire cutters from his utility belt and handed them to Archie.

"Thanks," said Archie, although he didn't say it with much enthusiasm.

"Do you have any idea which wire to cut?" Vicki asked.

"Not a clue."

"I once saw a TV movie where two guys were trying to figure out which wire to cut," offered Larryboy. "The star of the show cut the red wire and that defused the bomb."

Archie started to cut the red wire.

"NO, WAIT!" Larryboy shouted just in

time to stop him. "I just remembered. The colors on my TV were messed up that day. I think the red wire was really blue. They cut the BLUE wire to defuse the bomb."

Archie started to cut the blue wire.

"NO, WAIT!" Larryboy shouted just in time. "Actually, I had my TV repaired on the morning that I saw the movie. I think the red wire was red after all. Cut the red wire."

Archie started to cut the red wire.

"NO, WAIT!" Larryboy shouted. "I just remembered. The TV I owned at that time was a black-and-white set. Very retro. I have no idea which color wire the hero cut."

"I once heard that villains always use blue wires to detonate their bombs," interjected Tourist-Man. "That way, they always remember which wire sets off an explosion. Blue causes **KA-BLOOEY**. Get it?"

Sighing, Archie began to cut the blue wire.

As Archie paused for one terrifying moment before he snipped the wire, Tourist-Man exclaimed, "I've got to get this historic event on film. SAY CHEESE!"

FLASH!

The flash burst in Archie's face at the precise moment when the asparagus was cutting the blue wire.

The result?

Well, let's just say that Archie's wire cutters slipped a little.

Okay, they slipped A LOT.

Archie accidentally cut BOTH WIRES!

"This is not good," he said.

Everyone took a quick look at the timer to see what would happen. The clock had changed! Instead of one hour before the pop-can explosion, the timer switched to five seconds.

Five measly seconds.

CHAPTER 13

5...4...3...2...1...

Pop!

FIZZZZZZZZZZZZZZZZZZZZ
ZZZZZZZZZZZZZZZ!

KA-BLOOEY!

CHAPTER 14

VOLCANIC VILLAINY

A lot of the First Class superheroes were innocently frolicking on the beach when the underground explosion rocked the island. The pop-can explosion set off small earthquakes and created large waves.

Sweet Potato was about to take a bite of her cotton candy when the ground suddenly lurched.

She stumbled face-first into her cotton candy, couldn't see where she was going, and fell onto American Pie's lawn chair.

American Pie was catapulted out into the water, where he knocked Lemon Twist off of her surfboard.

Lemon Twist landed on top of the Scarlet Tomato, who was trying to drive a jet ski.

Blinded, the Scarlet Tomato ran his jet ski up on the beach, destroying Electro-Melon's sand castle.

Electro-Melon dove out of the way, landing on the end of a large table covered with cake, chips, punch, little hot dogs, and all kinds of silverware.

About a hundred dessert forks shot up into the air like silver arrows and rained down on a stack of inflatable inner tubes.

The inner tubes popped and shot all over the place, while people screamed, fell, and tried to dodge falling chunks of cake.

You get the idea.

Meanwhile, on the opposite side of the island, in a deserted cove, Coconut stood all alone on a beach. His escape pod was anchored in the water, a short distance away. Like everyone else, Coconut had felt the force of the underground explosion.

"What in the world?" he said. "The pop can wasn't supposed to explode for another hour."

Looking at the tip-top of Mount Superhero, Coconut saw a black cloud of smoke pour from the crater like a genie from a bottle. The volcano hadn't erupted yet, but it wouldn't be long before the mountain blew its lid.

"Where's Chili Pepper?" Coconut fretted. "He was supposed to be here a half hour ago! We need to get off this island. Fast!"

At that moment, a giant rock came hurtling toward Coconut like a meteor. Spotting it just in time, Coconut rolled to the side as the rock crashed into the sand.

"Whew! That was a close one," Coconut said, leaning against the rock and wiping his forehead with a handkerchief.

He didn't notice as the rock slowly opened two eyes—two very *angry* eyes.

"What are ya doing messin' with my volcano?" snarled the volcanic rock.

At the sound of the rock's voice, Coconut leaped ten feet forward and spun around. "I...We...I...didn't know it was your volcano."

"Well, now you know," said the rock. "You can tell your little chili friend the same thing." The rock skipped across the water and hopped into the cockpit of Chili Pepper's escape pod.

"Hey, you can't take that submarine! That's ours!" Coconut made a mad dash toward the boulder, but the rock monster sent out a blistering stream of bad breath, knocking Coconut backwards.

Revving the engine, the mysterious rock steered the escape pod into deeper water, then disappeared under the surface, leaving behind only a cloud of bubbles—and one very confused Coconut.

CHAPTER 15

SURF'S UP, DUDE!

Back in the underground tunnels...

When the pop can opened, a huge stream of Chili-Cola exploded from the earth, hitting Veggies like water from a fire hose and hurling them backwards. But because Chili-Cola is cold and refreshing, the Veggies survived the drenching. They simply felt...sticky...

...and very angry...at Tourist-Man.

"Will you knock it off with the pictures!" Bob shouted, furious that Tourist-Man's incessant flash had caused Archie to cut both wires.

"No wonder you were voted off the other side of the island!" Vicki snapped. "Look what you've done!"

"Maybe we should vote on whether Tourist-Man gets to stay on our side of the island," suggested Larryboy.

"Don't you think you're being a bit harsh, Master Larry?" Archie asked.

"Anyone who wants me off the island, raise your hand," Tourist-Man offered, glancing around. "OK, no hands—I stay."

"Very funny," said Bob. "We don't have hands. Let's vote on paper."

Bob tore pieces of paper from his notebook and passed them around for the vote. It was unanimous. Tourist-Man was booted from the Second Class side of the island. He was stunned, speechless. For the first time since they had met him, his big grin had vanished. "You're kicking me off this side of the island, too?"

"I guess we are. Sorry. It's a matter of survival."

Tourist-Man's face wore the saddest expression they had ever seen. Piling his three giant pieces of luggage on his back, Tourist-Man slowly turned and trudged away. A couple of times, he paused to throw a sad look over his shoulder.

The group could hear him sniff as he wandered off in the opposite direction.

"Gee. Maybe we were a little too hard on him," Larryboy said after Tourist-Man had disappeared into a tunnel.

"Yes, I believe we may have been," said Archie. "Maybe we—"

But there was no time for regrets now. A heavy-duty earthquake suddenly rose up from the depths of the cave, knocking everyone to the ground. Cracks opened up in the cave floor and spread like fast-growing, flaming fingers. Red-hot chili spurted and bubbled through the cracks, flooding the tunnel with extra-spicy chili sauce!

Bob, Archie, Larryboy, and Vicki could hear the roar of something approaching them from the tunnel.

"The chili is headed our way!" shouted Larryboy. "Run for it!"

They hadn't gone very far when a wall of glowing hot chili suddenly poured into the cavern, flooding the entire tunnel. There was no way they were going to outrun this wave of burning liquid.

But that's when they heard a voice. **"KAWABUNGA, BABY!"**

It was Tourist-Man. He was on a surfboard riding a wave of chili right toward them. Equally amazing, he had balanced his three pieces of luggage on his head.

"Hop on, dudes!" he shouted.

Tourist-Man's surfboard had two tiny engines strapped to its bottom. But even niftier, he steered the surfboard using a device that looked like the controls for a video game.

The Veggies scrambled up to a ledge and leaped aboard. They landed on top of the luggage, which was still balanced on Tourist-Man's head. However, Larryboy couldn't quite fit on the luggage, so he wound up on top of Bob.

They raced through the huge cavern looking like something from a circus act, scraping the ceiling as they went.

"Where did you get this surfboard?" Larryboy yelled over the roar of the rushing chili.

"It was in one of my suitcases!" Tourist-Man shouted back. "I carry doohickeys—they're what make me a superhero!"

"We're sorry we voted you off our side of the island," shouted Archie. "You didn't have to come back to rescue us, but you did. You're a true superhero, Tourist-Man!"

"Thanks!"

Then the surfing Veggies hit a big dip as the river of chili roared downhill.

"AHHHHHHHHHHHHHHHHHHHH!"

It was like being on an amusement park ride gone berserk. A sharp right turn nearly toppled Larryboy from the top of the stack. If he hadn't fired a suction cup onto Bob's shiny head, Larryboy would have gone flying off and hit the wall.

"Oh my," Archie said, looking down at the surfboard.

"Oh my," was right. Archie was the first to notice that the acid-hot chili was slowly eating away at the surfboard. The board was now about one-third its original size.

Making things even more complicated, the cave narrowed up ahead with stalactites hanging from the ceiling like razor-sharp needles.

Larryboy had no choice. He had to leap from the top of Bob's head to keep from being shish-kebabed on the end of one of the daggerlike rocks. Still connected to Bob's head by his supersuction plunger, Larryboy wound up being pulled behind.

When Tourist-Man took a sharp left, Larryboy was flung around like the tail end in a crack-the-whip game. His tether cord wrapped around a stalactite, caught, and then ripped the deadly rock from the ceiling.

Bob ducked as the stalactite went whistling over his head, followed close behind by Larryboy.

"Hi, Bob! Bye, Bob," chirped Larryboy as he sailed just inches over Bob's noggin.

By this time, the chili had eaten away even more of the surfboard. It was now about half its original size—barely big enough to hold the Veggies.

"I think we're past the worst of it!" shouted Archie.

Wrong!

Just then, the volcano erupted.

KA-BLOOEY!

CHAPTER 16

HOT, HOT, HOT!

A geyser of chili lifted the tiny surfboard,
pushing it up, up, up through a vertical shaft in the
volcano. Larryboy, still attached to Bob's head by his
plunger, trailed close behind.

"Top floor, please," Tourist-Man said, as if in an
elevator, shooting up through a tall building.

A second later, the angry mountain spit them out of
its top, hurling them high into the air. Of course, what
goes up must come down. But it was a long way
down!

"We're goners," yelled Bob, as their free fall
began.

"Never say goner when I've still got
luggage handy," said Tourist-Man,
completely unruffled.

He pushed a button on his remote control, and his second piece of luggage popped open. Inside, a hang glider automatically unfolded.

The group clutched onto the glider as Tourist-Man steered it through a shower of erupting chili and blobs of sizzling hot cheese, which shot from the top of Mount Superhero.

Down on the island, the exclusive resort was in flames. None of the superheroes cared any longer who was First or Second Class, who was a servant, or who had what special powers.

Disasters have a way of putting everyone in the same boat—in this case, a sinking boat.

Lava-hot chili consumed buildings in its fiery flow. Giant, stale dinner rolls crashed through roofs. Shredded cheese fell from on high like gooey ash, gunking up everything in sight.

The island looked like a giant food fight.

By this time, most of the superheroes had attempted to escape by boat, helicopter, plane, jet-pack, or by simply flying on their own steam. But every one of them hit an invisible force field—like birds flying into a windowpane.

They were trapped on Superhero Island.

Tourist-Man brought the hang glider down in a cove, which just happened to be the spot where Coconut was waiting for Chili Pepper.

"Stay right where you are, Coconut!" shouted Larryboy, running toward the thug. "We know Chili Pepper was behind this volcanic eruption! So tell us how to get off this island. You and the Snooty Gourmet must have an escape route."

Coconut didn't say a word.

Larryboy aimed a supersuction ear at the hooligan. "If you don't tell us, I've got a chili-filled plunger with your name on it."

"Okay, okay," said Coconut. "I'll tell you anything, but please no more chili! I've had enough!"

"How do we get off the island?" Larryboy repeated.

"There's a hole in the invisible force field about 100 feet below the surface of the ocean and about a half mile away from this beach."

Coconut handed a map to Larryboy, showing exactly how to locate the underwater hole in the force field. "Here, I won't need it anyway. Chili and I don't have a way to reach the escape hole anymore."

"You didn't plan your escape very carefully," said

Larryboy. "You've trapped yourselves on the island, too."

"Our escape pod was stolen by a huge rock with angry eyes," grumbled Coconut. "Now can I leave? I think Chili is still somewhere on the island. I've got to find him!"

"Sure, go ahead."

As Coconut took off for the center of the burning island, the group was left with two burning questions: How were they going to reach the hole in the force field if it was deep underwater? And how were they going to save the other superheroes?

All eyes turned to Tourist-Man, who had one piece of luggage left.

CHAPTER 17

THERE'S A HOLE
IN THE BOTTOM OF THE SEA

"Of course I have scuba

gear," said Tourist-Man matter-of-factly.

"I also have a submersible jet ski. Will that

help?"

With another push of a button, Tourist-Man's

third piece of luggage popped open, revealing a

submersible jet ski and miniature breathing tanks.

"Who says that heroes who use doohickeys and

gadgets aren't important?" said Vicki, with a big grin.

"Right-O!" smiled Larryboy. "Here's the plan, guys.

Tourist-Man, can you use the map and your doohickeys

to get Bob, Vicki, and Archie safely through the hole

in the force field?"

"Yes," agreed Tourist-Man. "But aren't you

coming with us?"

Larryboy tried to strike a dramatic pose, but it was hard to do when little streams of chili were pouring onto the beach. He kept dancing around the sizzling streams.

"Drat," said Larryboy. "Forget the dramatic pose. I'm heading back to the center of the island. Someone needs to tell the other superheroes how to get out of here! We've got to include them in our plan!"

"You're willing to do that for superheroes who thought they were better than you all week?" Archie asked. "A lot of people wouldn't be willing to risk their necks for people like that."

"EVERYONE is just as important as the other in God's eyes. And I don't have a neck," Larryboy pointed out.

"That's the spirit!" Archie beamed.

Then Larryboy recited the words from the Superhero Handbook: "Don't be proud. Be willing to be a friend of people who aren't considered important. Don't think you are better than others."

With that, Larryboy dashed to the center of the inferno, knowing full well that he might be giving up his only hope of escape.

CHAPTER 18

TARZAN OF THE VEGGIES

Burning-hot chili was everywhere. In fact, once Larryboy got past the beach, the edge of the jungle was as far as he could go. The entire jungle floor was covered with chili. There was no way to get past the hot liquid to the resort, where the other superheroes were trapped.

Unless…

"Tarzan, eat your heart out!" Larryboy yelled.

Larryboy used his supersuction ears to leap from branch to branch in the tropical rain forest. **"AHHHH-U-AHHHHH-U-AHHHHH-U...ACK!"** he coughed as he tried to do the Tarzan yell, nearly choking on smoke gushing out of the volcano.

At the resort, Larryboy located the Larrymobile, but he found it covered in a thick layer of melted cheese.

"Drat," the caped cucumber said.

"Need some help?" said a voice.

Larryboy looked up to see Lemon Twist. Behind her were his old pals, the Scarlet Tomato, Electro-Melon, and Sweet Potato.

"Sorry we acted like we were more important than ya'll this week," said Sweet Potato, with Electro-Melon and Lemon Twist nodding in agreement.

"The same-a here," added the Scarlet Tomato.

"I guess it's easy to think you're better than others. But the fact is, we're not," added Electro-Melon.

"Thanks," said Larryboy. "But we don't have much time. Can you guys help me get this cheese off the Larrymobile?"

"My uncle Guido could-a probably eat all of that-a cheese," said the Scarlet Tomato. "But he's-a on a low-fat diet now, and my-a aunt Laverne wouldn't-a let him even look at this-a much cheese-a. He tries-a to raid the refrigerator every night, which is why—"

"Sorry, S.T., but we don't have time to hear about it," said Lemon Twist. Without another word, the twisting lemon powered up her tornado winds and literally blew the cheese off of the Larrymobile.

"Thanks, Lemon Twist," said Larryboy. "Now, here's my plan..."

Twenty minutes later, Larryboy and the other 133 superheroes were crowded onto one of the last remaining pieces of island not covered with hot chili or cheese. Wearing scuba gear borrowed from the resort's sport shop, the superheroes were connected to the Larrymobile by 133 water-ski ropes.

"Can the Larrymobile pull this many water-skiers at the same time?" asked Sweet Potato.

"Time to find out," said Electro-Melon.

Larryboy pushed a yellow button on his control panel, and the Larrymobile instantly transformed into the Larryboat. The purple speedboat tore off across the burning chili with 133 superheroes trailing behind—each one trying to water-ski on chili without getting their ropes tangled or their costumes fried.

Larryboy raced straight for the ocean. As he did, the entire island began to snap, crackle, and pop. The chili was so hot that it ate away at the water skis. But just before the Larryboat and the skiers became completely cooked, they reached the cool, refreshing water of the ocean.

At the edge of the sea, Larryboy pushed the orange button, and the Larrymobile changed from a boat to a submarine. Diving beneath the surface of the sea, the Larrysubmarine continued to pull the water-skiers along. Only they were now *underwater skiers* using their scuba gear.

As the Larrysubmarine raced through the underwater hole in the force field, Superhero Island sank into the sea and completely vanished from sight.

It was gone. **KAPUT!**

It was almost as if Superhero Island had never even existed.

CHAPTER 19

SOMETHING'S R.O.T.T.E.N.

Three days

later, back in Bumblyburg, in a secret

hideout beneath the Bumble Hotel, one

of the most dastardly meetings of all time

was being held. It was the monthly meeting

of that exclusive but diabolical club known as

R.O.T.T.E.N.—the League of Really Ornery and

Terribly Tacky Evildoers who are very Naughty.

The most infamous villains in all of Veggiedom

were there, including Awful Alvin and his sidekick

Lampy, Outback Jack, the Emperor, the Alchemist and

Mother Pearl, Greta Von Gruesome, and the Iceberg and

his Snow Peas.

The mysterious rock was also there. In fact,

this creature was in the process of asking to be

admitted as a new member of the R.O.T.T.E.N.

Club. And that wasn't easy. You had to be a really rotten vegetable.

Which raised a good question. Should they let a rock monster join a club for vegetables only?

"So I lured all of the superheroes to my island by playing up to their pride," the boulder explained in his speech to the League Membership Committee. "I told the superheroes they should spend their vacation on an exclusive island specially designed for the best of the best—themselves! They bought it—hook, line, and sinker!"

The **R.O.T.T.E.N.** committee members nodded, smiled, and snickered.

"But how did you handle that meddling cucumber Larryboy?" asked Mother Pearl.

"That was easy," said the rock. "I separated Larryboy from the other heroes by sending him to the Second Class beach—a beach for superheroes without special powers. I figured he couldn't cause trouble if he was cut off from the others."

The villains exchanged smiles of approval.

"Once the superheroes were at my resort, I triggered a force field that trapped them on the island. And then I set off a volcanic eruption that would've made Mount Vesuvius seem like a picnic. Now I am happy to announce that over 130 superheroes have all been destroyed!"

A gasp arose from the villains on the R.O.T.T.E.N. committee.

"I was wondering where all of the superheroes were hiding the past week," said Awful Alvin. "This is cause for a celebration! Dance with me, Lampy!"

"Does that mean I'm evil enough for your organization?" the rock asked proudly. "Can a boulder join the rancid ranks of R.O.T.T.E.N.?"

The Emperor, a small but powerful cherry tomato, banged a gavel on the table. "Anyone who can do what you have just done deserves to be a member of R.O.T.T.E.N.—even if you are a rock. All in favor of making him a member give an evil cackle."

Every single villain responded with an evil cackle.

The Emperor banged his gavel once again. "It's unanimous. Rocky, you are the newest member of the exclusive R.O.T.T.E.N. Club. Bring out the food, and let's party!"

From a back room, a tall waiter wheeled out a huge platter of food covered with a silver lid.

"A toast to the end of all superheroes!" shouted the

Emperor, holding up his glass of soda.

"And a toast to the ARREST of all supervillains!" came another voice. However, this voice came from under the lid of the food platter.

The waiter lifted the lid, revealing none other than LARRYBOY. The plunger-headed hero raised a piece of toast in the air and then sprang into action. He fired a plunger at the boulder, while superheroes poured into the room from all sides.

Some superheroes crashed through the ceiling, sliding down on ropes. Others popped out of closets. Still others leaped out of the air duct vents in the walls.

"I thought you said you destroyed every superhero?" Iceberg shouted at the rock.

"I did!" blasted back the boulder. "You have to believe me!"

"Why should anyone believe you?" declared Larryboy. "You aren't even who you say you are."

Then, in the most dramatic moment of all, Larryboy used one of his supersuction ears to reveal that the rock monster was simply wearing a costume. Yanking off the costume was a stunning surprise!

Inside was none other than Chili Pepper.

CHAPTER 20

A PICTURE-PERFECT POSTCARD ENDING

The raid on **R.O.T.T.E.N.** set the record for the largest number of supervillain arrests in a single day. To celebrate a few weeks later, Tourist-Man invited all of the superheroes to his home to watch his slide show of vacation pictures. Over 100 superheroes gathered to watch his slides. Roughly 80 of them, however, were sound asleep.

"How can Tourist-Man make *this* vacation seem boring?" Vicki whispered.

"I don't know. Just his special talent, I guess," Larry the Janitor said.

The vacation on Superhero Island had included defusing bombs, surfing on hot lava-chili, being hurled out of an erupting volcano, and escaping through an underwater passage. But somehow, some way, Tourist-Man's slides were still dreadfully dull.

"And this is me buttoning my shirt," he said, showing a photo of his Hawaiian shirt. "And this is a close-up of the button. And here's…"

"By the way, where's Larryboy?" asked Vicki when the slide show mercifully came to an end.

"Gee, that's a good question."

Vicki had invited Larry the Janitor to be her escort to the party, since they never did get a chance to finish their picnic together. So our cucumber hero came as Larry, not Larryboy.

At first, Tourist-Man wasn't going to let Larry the Janitor come to the party, since—after all—he wasn't a superhero. But then Tourist-Man remembered what it was like to be left out. So he welcomed Larry with open arms (or at least he would've if he had arms).

"Larryboy's not here. So I guess you're just stuck with me—an unimportant janitor," Larry said to Vicki.

"Unimportant janitor? How can you say that? EVERYONE is important in God's eyes," Vicki responded. And then she gave him a big grin. "Besides, you're just the way I like you."

Larry the Janitor beamed.

At that moment, Sweet Potato leaned over and said, "Hey, I never did hear how ya'll figured out that Chili Pepper disguised himself as a rock."

"It was his breath," Vicki said. "Larryboy realized that Chili Pepper's bad breath was just like the dangerously spicy breath of the mysterious rock."

"But why did Chili Pepper even need a disguise?" asked Sweet Potato.

"Because Chili desperately wanted to become a member of R.O.T.T.E.N.," interjected Bob the Tomato.

"That's right," said Vicki. "Bob and I discovered that about a year ago, Chili Pepper tried to join the R.O.T.T.E.N. Club, but they wouldn't let him in. They said he wasn't evil enough to join their club. Being left out like that, he felt really rejected."

"So Chili Pepper came up with the boulder disguise and devised the most evil plot he could think of—destroying almost every superhero in the world with something he loved the most," said Bob. "If that didn't get him into the R.O.T.T.E.N. Club, nothing would."

"His plot had one other advantage," added Vicki. "Chili thought that Coconut would ruin his chances of making it into the R.O.T.T.E.N. Club. So he decided to ditch

Coconut by disguising himself as a rock and abandoning his sidekick on the island."

"The disguise also gave him a secret identity to use while he was stealing scuba gear and other supplies for his resort," Bob noted.

"Diabolical," gasped Sweet Potato. "I wonder what ever happened to Coconut."

Good question.

For an answer, let's go to the other side of Bumblyburg, where Chili Pepper was locked away in the Jail for the Criminally Snobby. On this particular day, one of the prison guards had brought him a particularly odd postcard.

"Mail for Chili Pepper!" announced the guard, sneaking a peek at the postcard.

"Give that to me," Chili Pepper snarled, snatching it from the guard. Burning with curiosity, Chili flipped over the postcard, and this is what he read:

Dear Chili:

Weather is good. Wish you were here. I just wanted to give you my great news. When Superhero Island sank into the ocean, I SURVIVED!

When the island sank, I climbed onto a giant dinner roll and drifted at sea for a week before being picked up by a ship. So don't worry, I'll be waiting for you when you get out of jail. See you soon!

Your sidekick and faithful friend,

Coconut

Coconut was back? Chili Pepper couldn't believe it. His eyes bulged. Steam came out of his ears. He turned red in the face. And then...

"AHHHHHHHHHHHHHHHHHHHHHHHHHHHHHH!"

Chili Pepper exploded in anger. He flipped his lid.

You might even say he erupted.

THE END

LarryBoy Versus the Volcano!
Softcover 978-0-310-70728-8

The Good, the Bad and the Eggly
LarryBoy Cartoon DVD

BOOKS

LarryBoy and the Emperor of Envy (Book 1)
Softcover 978-0-310-70467-6

LarryBoy and the Awful Ear Wacks Attacks (Book 2)
Softcover 978-0-310-70468-3

LarryBoy and the Sinister Snow Day (Book 3)
Softcover 978-0-310-70561-1

LarryBoy and the Yodelnapper (Book 4)
Softcover 978-0-310-70562-8

LarryBoy and the Good, the Bad, and the Eggly (Book 5)
Softcover 978-0-310-70650-2

LarryBoy in the Attack of Outback Jack (Book 6)
Softcover 978-0-310-70649-6

LarryBoy and the Amazing Brain-Twister (Book 7)
Softcover 978-0-310-70651-9

LarryBoy and the Abominable Trashman (Book 8)
Softcover 978-0-310-70652-6

LarryBoy Versus the Volcano (Book 9)
Softcover 978-0-310-70728-8

LarryBoy and the Snowball of Doom (Book 10)
Softcover 978-0-310-70729-5

DVDS

The Angry Eyebrows
LarryBoy Cartoon DVD

Leggo My Ego
LarryBoy Cartoon DVD

The Yodelnapper
LarryBoy Cartoon DVD

The Good, the Bad, and the Eggly
LarryBoy Cartoon DVD

LarryBoy and the Rumor Weed
VeggieTales DVD

LarryBoy & the Fib from Outer Space
VeggieTales DVD

LarryBoy and the Bad Apple
VeggieTales DVD